LITTLE DRAGGIN' BEAR

The Cat on Wheels

INSPIRING ANIMALS

LEIA TAIT

Weigl Publishers Inc.

Published by Weigl Publishers Inc.
350 5th Avenue, Suite 3304, PMB 6G
New York, NY 10118-0069

Website: www.weigl.com

Library of Congress Cataloging-in-Publication Data

Tait, Leia
  Little Draggin' Bear: inspiring animals/ Leia Tait.
                    p. cm.
  Includes index.
  ISBN: 978-1-59036-861-9 (soft cover: alk. Paper) –
  ISBN: 978-1-59036-860-2 (hard cover: alk. Paper)
  1. Little Draggin' Bear (CAT) – Juvenile literature.
  2. Cats—Oregan—Ashland—Biography—Juvenile literature. I.
Title.
  SF445.7.T35 2009
  636.8092'9—dc22

2008015574

Printed and bound in the United States of America
1 2 3 4 5 6 7 8 9 0   12 11 10 09 08

PHOTO CREDITS:

Courtesy of Dr. Alice M. Sievers: pages 1, 3, 4, 6 top, 7, 10, 12, 13,
15, 16 bottom, 17, 20, 21
Getty Images: pages 6 bottom, 8, 9, 14 top, 16 top, 19

Every reasonable effort has been made to trace ownership
and to obtain permission to reprint copyright material. The
publishers would be pleased to have any errors or omissions
brought to their attention so that they may be corrected in
subsequent printings.

Editor: Heather Hudak
Design: Terry Paulhus
Consultant: Dr. Alice M. Sievers

Contents

13

20

Who is Little Draggin' Bear?

Little Draggin' Bear is a cat. He belongs to Alice Sievers. Alice is a veterinarian, or animal doctor. She adopted Little Draggin' Bear in 2004, when he was a kitten.

Draggin' Bear is a **paraplegic**. He cannot move his back legs. They are **paralyzed** from an injury when he was a kitten. Draggin' Bear still leads a full life. He runs, plays, and has fun. He is an inspiration to many people.

Draggin' Bear lives with Alice and her husband, Gordon, in Oregon. He spends most of his time with Alice at Bear Creek Animal Clinic. This is an animal hospital that Alice owns.

Draggin' Bear is a happy cat that has overcome a huge challenge.

Learning to Change When Draggin' Bear lost the use of his back legs, his life changed. He had to learn to do things differently. Imagine losing the use of your legs. How would your life change? What challenges would you face?

Bear Creek Animal Clinic is located in Ashland, Oregon. This is a small city in Oregon's mountains. It is about 15 miles (24 kilometers) north of the California border. About 20,000 people live in Ashland.

Ashland is known for its historic buildings and excellent schools. It is home to the Oregon Shakespeare Festival.

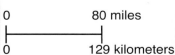

A Difficult Beginning

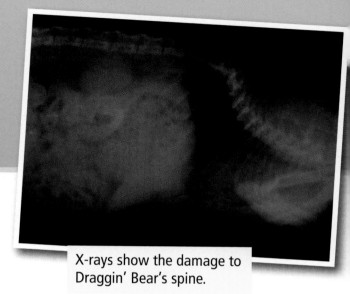

X-rays show the damage to Draggin' Bear's spine.

As a kitten, Little Draggin' Bear was a stray. He lived outdoors, near an apartment building. Draggin' Bear and his brothers and sisters had no one to look after them.

One day, Little Draggin' Bear was attacked by a raccoon. The raccoon broke Draggin' Bear's spine. Draggin' Bear's legs stopped working. He could not walk.

A young man found Little Draggin' Bear. He brought the kitten to Bear Creek Animal Clinic. There, Alice cared for Draggin' Bear. She did some tests and saw that his back was broken. He was very tiny. Draggin' Bear weighed only 1 pound (0.5 kilograms).

Most raccoons are about the same size as a house cat.

Alice nursed Draggin' Bear back to health. He soon doubled in size. However, Alice could not fix Draggin' Bear's back. He would always be paralyzed.

Meet Alice Sievers

Alice has been a veterinarian since 2000. At the Bear Creek Animal Clinic, she examines animals and gives **vaccinations** to help them stay healthy. She treats sick and injured animals, like Draggin' Bear. Alice and the clinic staff named Little Draggin' Bear for the way he moves. Draggin' Bear uses his front legs to pull his body around, dragging his back legs behind him. "Bear" was chosen for the name of Alice's clinic, Bear Creek, and because the cat looks like a gray bear.

All about Cats

Breeds

Domestic, or house, cats are related to lions, tigers, and other large cats. House cats are the smallest cats in the world. They can be many colors and shapes. There are about 40 house cat breeds. They all share the same basic features. Draggin' Bear is a mixed breed. He has medium-length gray hair and a long, fluffy tail.

Kitten

Adult

Cats are full grown at one year of age. Most house cats weigh about 10 pounds (4.5 kg). They are independent animals. Cats are fast, strong, and **agile**. They are very smart. Most house cats live for about 16 years.

Newborn kittens rely on their mother. Their eyes are closed until they are about 10 days old. Newborn kittens spend most of their time sleeping and drinking milk from their mother. After about four weeks, kittens learn to walk. They are curious and love to explore. They enjoy chasing balls, strings, or ribbons. Over time, kittens become more **independent**.

A Closer Look

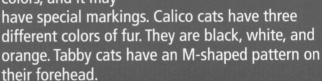

Eyes

Cats have large eyes. In low light, their pupils grow large and round, letting in more light. This helps cats see well in the dark. Cats have a third eyelid, called a haw. The haw protects the cat's eyes from light and dust.

Fur

Most cats have fur on their bodies to keep them warm. The fur may be many colors, and it may have special markings. Calico cats have three different colors of fur. They are black, white, and orange. Tabby cats have an M-shaped pattern on their forehead.

Toes

Most cats have five toes on their front paws and four toes on their back paws. Cats walk on their toes. Each toe has a sharp claw. Most often, these claws are hidden. They extend when a cat spreads its toes. Cats use their claws for protection.

Tail

A cat's tail is part of its backbone. Cats use their tails to balance. They swish, lift, and thump their tails to communicate. Only Manx cats have no tails. Draggin' Bear has a long, fluffy tail. Like his back legs, Draggin' Bear's tail is paralyzed. He cannot move it on his own.

Becoming a Star

A lice decided to adopt Draggin' Bear. She and Gordon wanted to help this special cat live a long and happy life. To begin, they made a cart to help him walk.

Gordon and Alice built a small cart to lift Draggin' Bear's back legs off the ground. They tried many designs. Finally, Alice and Gordon settled on a cart made from K'Nex™ toys. The cart's wheels made it easy for Draggin' Bear to walk and run. Draggin' Bear loved his new "wheelchair." When others saw Draggin' Bear in his wheelchair, they were amazed.

Draggin' Bear uses his wheelchair to run and play like other cats.

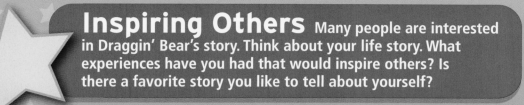
Newspapers, such as the *Medford Mail Tribune* in Oregon, wrote stories about Draggin' Bear. Television crews wanted to film him. Draggin' Bear became well known in his hometown.

Kitty Quiz

There are many amazing cats in the world. Read the list of names. Do you recognize any of these well-known cats? Research online to learn more about these cats. Now, read the list of their achievements. Match the cats to their achievements.

1. All Ball	a. sailed with explorers in the 1800s
2. Creme Puff	b. plays the piano
3. Fred	c. ran for president
4. Morris	d. was the oldest cat ever recorded
5. Nora	e. belonged to Koko the gorilla
6. Trim	f. worked undercover

Answers: 1. (e) All Ball was the pet kitten of Koko the gorilla. 2. (d) Creme Puff lived to be 38 years old—the oldest cat ever recorded. 3. (f) Fred worked undercover with the New York Police Department in 2006. 4. (c) Morris is a well-known cat who ran for president in 1988 and 1992. 5. (b) Nora is a cat from Philadelphia who can play the piano. 6. (a) Trim sailed with Matthew Flinders, the first explorer to sail around Australia.

Draggin' Bear
at Home

Draggin' Bear has had four wheelchairs.

Draggin' Bear has grown a great deal since Alice adopted him. As he grew, Alice and Gordon made new wheelchairs for him. When Draggin' Bear stopped growing, Alice bought him a wheelchair made just for cats. This chair is made from **aluminum**. It is very light, so Draggin' Bear can move around easily.

Draggin' Bear lives with Alice and Gordon in a house that is on one level. The house has wood floors. This makes it easy for Draggin' Bear to pull his wheelchair around. Sometimes, Draggin' Bear will topple his chair if he makes a sharp turn. He will wait for help from Alice, or he will slip out of the chair and scoot away on his front legs.

Each day after breakfast, Draggin' Bear goes to the Bear Creek Animal Clinic with Alice. He scoots about in his wheelchair, watching the day's events. In the afternoon, Draggin' Bear naps in Alice's office. He wakes up when it is time to go home for dinner. At night, Draggin' Bear sleeps in a cat bed or in the bottom level of a kitty condo. This is his own private space.

Draggin' Bear can sleep in his wheelchair, but some days he likes to rest without it.

Staying Healthy

To live the best life possible, it is important for Draggin' Bear to stay healthy. A nutritious diet helps him do this. Like other cats, Draggin' Bear eats dry and canned foods made just for cats. Dry kibble cleans and strengthens his teeth. Canned food contains **protein** and vitamins. Alice gives Draggin' Bear tasty treats that clean his teeth and freshen his breath.

Draggin' Bear eats a mix of wet and dry foods.

Having a vet for an owner helps keep Draggin' Bear in excellent health. Alice often looks in his mouth, eyes, and ears for signs of illness. She examines his belly for lumps, listens to the strength of his heart and lungs, and checks his skin.

Alice uses a stethoscope to listen to Draggin' Bear's heart.

14

Overcoming Obstacles

Draggin' Bear often needs help **grooming**. Unlike other cats, the claws on Draggin' Bear's back paws do not wear down from use. Alice trims his claws often. This is one of Draggin' Bear's least favorite activities. He does not like to hold still. Alice brushes Draggin' Bear to keep his fur clean. Sometimes, she gives him a bath.

Since Draggin' Bear cannot feel the back part of his body, he cannot use a litterbox like other cats. Instead, Draggin' Bear wears a diaper. Three to six times a day, Alice empties his bladder. Sometimes, she massages Draggin' Bear's **colon** to help him with a bowel movement.

Delightful Draggin' Bear

raggin' Bear does not know that he is different from other cats. He is just as happy, playful, and loving as any other cat. Draggin' Bear enjoys swatting at feathers and playing with cat toys. He loves to run very fast and skip or hop in his wheelchair. He has a scratching post that he enjoys clawing and climbing with his front paws.

Draggin' Bear loves attention from people. He likes when people pet him and scratch his ears. He especially enjoys cuddling.

Draggin' Bear likes to play with fuzzy mouse toys.

Draggin' Bear and his dog friend Magnus dress up at the clinic.

Getting Along
Draggin' Bear prefers people and cats to dogs, but he shares his home with Magnus the pug. Have you ever had to get along with someone you did not like? How did you do it?

Along with Draggin' Bear, Alice and Gordon have five other cats. Their names are Robin, Scooter, Turnip, Bitsy, and Trouble. Alice and Gordon also have a pug dog named Magnus. Draggin' Bear gets along well with the cats, but he does not like dogs.

A Special Friend

Little Draggin' Bear's favorite friend is Miss Hiss. Miss Hiss is a fluffy black cat. She was rescued from a raccoon trap in 2006. She now lives at Bear Creek Animal Clinic. Miss Hiss and Draggin' Bear love to play. They like to snuggle together during their afternoon nap.

Giving Back

Draggin' Bear is a source of joy at the Bear Creek Animal Clinic. He entertains visitors by zooming about in his wheelchair. He helps guests feel comfortable and calm. Many people ask to see Draggin' Bear when they bring their own pets in for a check-up. Some even stop by the clinic just to visit him.

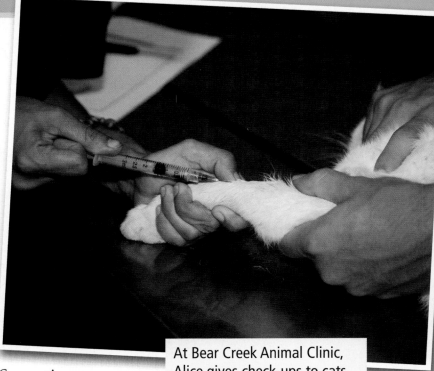

At Bear Creek Animal Clinic, Alice gives check-ups to cats and other animals.

Draggin' Bear helps visitors in other ways, too. Sometimes, he helps Alice show people how to give medicine to their pets. Other times, he helps people learn more about how a cat's body works.

Helping Others
Draggin' Bear enjoys helping others. Think about your own life. Is there something you can do, such as donating blood, that will help people in your community? Do some research with a parent or teacher. Then, do something you think will make a difference.

Most importantly, Draggin' Bear is an example of how animals with disabilities can live happy and healthy lives. He is an inspiration to pet owners and others around the world who call the clinic seeking support and advice.

Saving Lives

Once or twice a year, Draggin' Bear donates blood to ill or injured cats at the clinic. Without his donations, these cats might not become well. Draggin' Bear has donated blood to more than five cats. He has given these animals a second chance, much like Alice gave him.

Achievements and Successes

Draggin' Bear has been featured on television news programs, on websites, and in *Cat Fancy* magazine. He is truly a remarkable cat. Draggin' Bear does not let being paralyzed stop him from living a full life. He faces each new challenge with a positive spirit. Draggin' Bear has shown that, with hope and **perseverance**, it is possible to overcome great obstacles.

Draggin' Bear is an example for others, and he is also a great friend. His sweet and affectionate attitude brings joy to Alice, Gordon, and the staff and visitors at Bear Creek Animal Clinic. Draggin' Bear makes the world a happier place.

Draggin' Bear is very friendly, but he prefers to keep away from dogs.

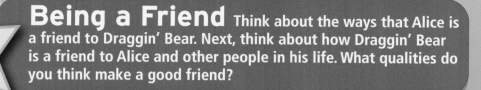

Being a Friend Think about the ways that Alice is a friend to Draggin' Bear. Next, think about how Draggin' Bear is a friend to Alice and other people in his life. What qualities do you think make a good friend?

Draggin' Bear is proof that everyone can lead a happy life. His differences do not hold him back. He helps others realize what they do best and inspires them to reach their own goals. Draggin' Bear's joy for life makes others feel good. His courage and kindness help save other animals. Draggin' Bear is a hero on wheels!

Draggin' Bear leads a healthy, happy life.

Design a Pet Wheelchair

Materials You Need:

- paper
- pencil
- crayons or felt markers
- construction toys
- stuffed animal or action figure

Instructions

Look at the pictures in this book. How would you design a wheelchair for paraplegic pets like Draggin' Bear?

On a sheet of paper, use a pencil to draw a simple wheelchair design. Be sure your design includes wheels, support for the pet's legs and hind end, and a way to keep the pet in the chair, such as a harness.

Label the different parts of your design. Use crayons or felt markers to color your drawing.

Using blocks, plastic wheels, and other building toys, make a model of the wheelchair you have designed.

Place a stuffed animal or action figure in your model to see if your design works. If parts of your wheelchair do not work, adjust either the design or the model. If the wheels do not turn, your toy falls out of the chair, or any part of your toy is dragging on the ground, try fixing these problems.

On another sheet of paper, write down the changes you make. When your design and model are complete, write a paragraph about why you think your design will work well.

Further Research

Many books and websites provide information about cats. To learn more about cats, borrow books from the library, or surf the Internet.

Books to Read
Most libraries have computers that connect to a database for researching information. If you input a key word, you will be provided with a list of books in the library that contain information on that topic. Non-fiction books are arranged numerically, using their call number. Fiction books are organized alphabetically by the author's last name.

Online Sites
To learn more about cats, check out http://animal.discovery.com/guides/cats/cats.html.

Read stories about other pet heroes at www.petswithdisabilities.org/stories.html.

To write to Draggin' Bear, visit www.dragginbear.com.

Glossary Index